The HOME Team
Toronto Maple Leafs®

Written by Holly Preston

Illustrated by James Hearne

Always Books Ltd.

The Home Team™: Toronto Maple Leafs®

The Home Team is a trademark of Always Books Ltd.

Text and illustrations © 2017 NHL
All Rights Reserved.

Manufactured by Friesens Corporation in Altona, MB, Canada
March 2017
Job # 230845

Library and Archives Canada Cataloguing in Publication

Preston, Holly, author
Toronto Maple Leafs / written by Holly Preston ; illustrated
by James Hearne.

(The home team)
ISBN 978-0-9951990-2-6 (softcover)

1. Toronto Maple Leafs (Hockey team)--Juvenile fiction.
I. Hearne, James, 1972-, illustrator II. Title. III. Series: Preston,
Holly. Home team

PS8631.R467T67 2017   jC813'.6   C2017-901128-6

Layout by James Hearne

For all young LEAFS™ fans
who know there's no team like ours!

There was nothing better than playing hockey ...

... except watching hockey when the **LEAFS** played.

Ben played forward. Liam played defence. Noah was in goal.
The boys played different positions. They had the same dream:
to one day play for the **MAPLE LEAFS**.

Even after playing all day, Ben dreamed only about hockey.

The only problem was Ben never scored. Ever.
The puck went high. The puck went low.
The puck went everywhere but where it was supposed to go.

How can I ever play for the **LEAFS**? Ben wondered.
His sister Sophia was the best goal scorer in the neighbourhood.

"The **LEAFS** were little boys once, too, Ben," his dad said.
"They didn't become hockey stars overnight."

His mom said, "You can learn a lot by watching what the **LEAFS** do."
She'd been a **LEAFS** fan forever.

The **LEAFS** are great skaters.

They make big plays.

They shoot. They score!

And make a million saves.

"The only way to get better is to practise," said Noah.
And so they practised hard. And then came the best suprise they'd ever had.
"We're going to a **LEAFS** game!" Liam yelled.

But at the game, the **LEAFS'** top scorer wasn't scoring at all!
"Something is wrong," said Ben.

The next day on the way to the rink, Ben found a shiny chain.
He put it on and ... he got a goal! And then another one!
"That's a good luck charm, for sure," Sophia said.

"Our player lost his good luck charm, kids," said Dad. "Maybe *that's* why he hasn't been scoring." The children knew hockey players were superstitious. They also knew where that charm was ...

... and what they had to do next!

Ben seized the moment.
"What does it take to play for the **MAPLE LEAFS**?" he asked.

Play like a team ...

... and with heart.

Never give up.

Believe in yourself.

"The **LEAFS** are the greatest team in the NHL," said Noah.
"We're going to be **LEAFS** fans forever," added Liam.

Everything was the way it should be.

All the next week Ben practised and practised.
He no longer had the good luck charm, but he had something else –
he believed in himself.

And that was all he really needed.

But Ben, like all hockey players, knew a little luck always helps ...

... especially when you're playing for the Stanley Cup®!

ABOUT THE AUTHOR

Holly Preston

Holly is a journalist who worked for CTV and CBC. She grew up watching NHL hockey with her brother and father. Now she creates children's picture books for professional sports teams and NCAA football fans. She hopes Leafs fans will enjoy having a book that celebrates their home team and encourages young fans to find a love of reading.

ABOUT THE ILLUSTRATOR

James Hearne

Born in London, England, James began his art career at the tender age of eight, selling drawings to guests at his grandparents' hotel. He continues to sell his whimsical illustrations around the globe as a full-time illustrator and full-time hockey fan.